ALICE AND THE PEACHES WILL DO ANYTHING
TO BEAT DONNA AND THE TURNIPS

Mr. Whipple, Alice's father, pointed at the display. "You cannot take these to school."

"But those are my campaign posters!" Alice said.

"Has your teacher seen these?"

"No. But she said it was okay for us to make posters and write slogans. She said it was a great idea. And I was the one who thought of it."

"Then I suggest you redo them. These slogans are libelous, Alice. Just listen to this." Mr. Whipple read them aloud.

"Only Dimwits Vote for Donna.

Up in the Air with Alice
Down in the Dumps with Donna.

Bookworms Make Bad Presidents."

Mr. Whipple stopped reading and glared at Alice.

"But, Daddy, what's wrong with them? They're just like the campaign ads on TV!"

"Alice!" Mr. Whipple said sharply. "This is *not* TV."

Bantam Skylark Books of related interest
Ask your bookseller for the books you have
  missed

Who Wants a Turnip for President, Anyway?

Laurie Adams and Allison Coudert

A BANTAM SKYLARK BOOK®
TORONTO · NEW YORK · LONDON · SYDNEY · AUCKLAND

For Alexa,
Caroline,
and Polly

RL 3, 008–011

WHO WANTS A TURNIP FOR PRESIDENT, ANYWAY?
A Bantam Skylark Book / September 1986

*Skylark Books is a registered trademark of Bantam Books, Inc.
Registered in U.S. Patent and Trademark Office and elsewhere.*

ISBN 0-553-15432-X

Published simultaneously in the United States and Canada

*Bantam Books are published by Bantam Books, Inc. Its trade-
mark, consisting of the words "Bantam Books" and the por-
trayal of a rooster, is Registered in U.S. Patent and Trademark
Office and in other countries. Marca Registrada. Bantam
Books, Inc., 666 Fifth Avenue, New York, New York 10103.*

PRINTED IN THE UNITED STATES OF AMERICA

S   0 9 8 7 6 5 4 3 2

Contents

CHAPTER ONE

Alice Plans Her Strategy

"*You? President?* Don't be ridiculous." Peter Hildreth stared at Alice Whipple. They were standing on the sidewalk in front of her apartment building. Alice was in the fifth grade at Miss Barton's School for Girls. Peter, her friend from across the street, went to the local public school. He was also a fifth grader.

"I'd like to know *why* you think it's ridiculous, Peter Hildreth?" Alice said, glaring at him. "It so happens that self-government at Miss Barton's starts in the fifth grade. That's the year we first elect class officers. And I intend to be elected president of my class." Alice put her nose right up against Peter's. She had to bend over a little because Peter was short for his age. "We've been studying the Constitution in American history," Alice continued. "And—"

"What's the Constitution?" interrupted Beatrice, Alice's younger sister. Beatrice was in the first grade. So was Peter's brother, James, who was quietly listening to the discussion.

1

Alice and Beatrice were both blond with short, straight hair and bangs. Their wide, mischievous eyes were blue. Alice had always been a bit chubby. Her parents said it was "baby fat" and that she would eventually outgrow it. Beatrice, who was quite slim, seemed to be able to eat as much as she wanted without gaining weight. Alice thought it was totally unfair that *she,* the elder sister, should be the one with the "baby fat."

Peter and James each had dark brown hair and lots of freckles.

"It's a document. An important historical document. You're too young to understand," Alice—who was still glaring at Peter—told Beatrice.

"Well, I suppose you might be elected president at a sissy school, but America has never had a girl president," Peter pointed out. Peter and James liked to tease Alice and Beatrice for going to an all-girls school where they had to wear uniforms.

The Miss Barton's uniform consisted of a dark blue tunic, skirt, and a blue or white shirt with a collar. The school blazer was maroon, with a yellow *B* and a small owl, the school symbol, inscribed in a circle on the front pocket. Peter and James sometimes referred to Alice and Beatrice as Miss Barton's Brats.

"When I'm grown-up, America will have a girl president," Alice declared. "This election is going to be good practice— Oh! Hi, Sarah," Alice yelled and waved as Sarah turned the corner.

Sarah Jamison had a mass of curly red hair framing her face. She was Alice's best friend at school.

"Here comes my campaign manager," said Alice. "She's running for vice-president, too."

Peter, James, and Beatrice watched Sarah hurry down the block toward them. Her curls bounced with each step.

"See you later, Peter," Alice said. "We have to plan our campaign strategy."

"Where's Lydia?" Alice whispered to Sarah as the three girls hung up their jackets in the hall of the Whipples' apartment.

"She's on her way."

"And Hilary?"

"I don't know. She was supposed to be here by now."

Mrs. Whipple called out from the kitchen. "Would you girls like a snack?" Mrs. Whipple taught reading four mornings a week. She liked to be home by the time her children were back from school.

"No, thank you," said Alice. "We've got some work to do."

"Yeah," said Beatrice.

"Well, if you change your minds, I'll be either in here or in the study."

Beatrice followed Alice and Sarah to Alice's room.

Alice hung a sign on her door: CAMPAIGN

HEADQUARTERS: NO ONE UNDER TEN AL-
LOWED IN.

"Read the sign," Alice told Beatrice.

Beatrice was just learning to read, and even
though she couldn't understand the first two
words, she could read the rest.

"That's not fair!" Beatrice protested.

"Sorry, Beatrice. No distractions. A presidential campaign is serious business, and we have
only one week to prepare ours. Not months or
even years like real politicians."

"Boring," said Beatrice. "I'm going to play
with Salisbury." Salisbury was Beatrice's turtle.

As Alice closed her door, the phone rang in
the kitchen.

"Alice!" called Mrs. Whipple a moment later,
"Telephone! I think it's Peter."

Alice ran from her room to the kitchen.

"Hello, Peter. What now? I'm very busy."
Alice was annoyed by the interruption.

"Well," said Peter, "I thought you might want
to know that an odd-looking girl is crouching behind the garbage cans in front of your building.
She has a ski mask pulled down over her face,
and she's wearing a duffle coat with the collar
turned up. I can see her from my window. She's
throwing paper airplanes at your window, but
they aren't reaching."

Peter's building was right across the street
from Alice's. His apartment was on the third
floor, and he could see the Whipples' kitchen from
his bedroom window.

"Thank you, Peter. Bye." Alice hung up and looked out the kitchen window. The Whipples' apartment was on the second floor.

"Lydia!" Alice yelled. "Come on in. I'll buzz you."

The Whipples' building did not have a doorman, so a visitor had to be identified over an intercom. The tenant would then open the main door by pushing a buzzer.

"Shhhh," whispered Lydia Spaulding. She glanced furtively over her shoulder and hurried into the vestibule of the building. When the buzzer rang, Lydia pushed the door open and rushed up the stairs. Since the Whipples were on the second floor, it was usually quicker to use the stairs than to wait for the elevator.

Alice opened the apartment door, and Lydia scooted inside.

"I didn't want to ring," Lydia said breathlessly. "Too conspicuous. Turnips could be staking out the house."

The fifth grade at Miss Barton's was divided into two cliques, the Peaches and the Turnips. A few girls were not included in either one. Alice, Sarah, and Lydia were Peaches, and Alice had been chosen the Peach candidate for class president that morning. The Turnips had their own candidates.

Mrs. Whipple poked her head out of the kitchen. "Hello, Lydia. I didn't hear you ring. Why on earth are wearing that ski mask and heavy coat? It's sixty-five degrees today!"

* * *

"Okay, Lydia. What's going on?" demanded Alice when they were back in her room with Sarah.

"You can't be too careful in politics," replied Lydia, whose long, black ponytail got messed up when she removed her ski mask. "I saw a Turnip crossing the street on my way over here." Lydia looked around the room. "Are you sure this place isn't bugged? Where's Hilary?"

"She's not here yet. And don't be ridiculous," Alice said, answering both questions at once. "Of course I'm sure. Now, let's get down to planning our strategy."

"You'll need an undercover operation," said Lydia. "All campaigns have one. I've decided to run yours. In fact, I've got a name all picked out. What do you think of A-P-E-S?"

Alice was puzzled. "That spells apes."

"It's the initials, of course. They stand for Alice for President Espionage System. Don't you think it sounds good? Every important organization has initials that spell something."

"But what will you *do*, Lydia?" Sarah inquired.

"Well, you know. Basically there are three techniques used in undercover work. Pranks is one. We could put powder in Donna's shoes during gym class to make her hair fall out."

Donna Ellington was the Turnip who had been nominated to run against Alice. Jane Fulton was Donna's running mate.

"That's silly," said Sarah. "What would we want to do that for?"

"No, it isn't. My father said the CIA tried to do that to Fidel Castro so he wouldn't have long hair and a beard. No one wants a bald president. Especially if he's a girl! We'll need an informer and a counterspy," continued Lydia. "And then there's blackmail and bribery."

"But Mrs. Parker says we should have a platform," Alice reminded her.

Mrs. Parker was the fifth-grade history and homeroom teacher.

"And Mrs. Parker says bribery is not allowed."

"Well, that's how Donna got Marina over to her side this afternoon," Lydia declared.

Alice and Sarah gasped. Marina was a Peach. Peaches were supposed to be loyal.

"Marina voting for a Turnip! But that's treason!" wailed Sarah. "Who would think it of a Peach!"

"How did Donna do it?" Alice demanded.

"She used her brother," explained Lydia. "You know how tall Marina is. And she thinks she's so great because she's the only one in the class who wears a bra. Well, Donna's brother is *tall*, and he's in the *sixth* grade. Donna told Marina she'd get her brother to take her to the fifth-grade square dance if she voted for her instead of you."

"That's terrible," said Alice.

"Shhhh!" Lydia put her finger to her lips.

She tiptoed over to the door and suddenly jerked it open. Beatrice fell into the room.

"Beatrice!" Alice exclaimed.

"You see," said Lydia triumphantly. "I told you. Spies wherever you turn."

"Get out, Beatrice," said Alice sternly. "We don't want you here."

"But, Alice—"

"No 'buts.'" Alice began pushing Beatrice out the door.

"But I know a secret. I do, Alice. It's about Cynthia." Cynthia was a Turnip.

"We're busy, Beatrice."

"Wait. Let her talk," advised Lydia.

Beatrice began. "Yesterday I was at Cynthia's house playing with her sister. She's in my class. Cynthia got a thirty-two on the last math test."

Alice, Sarah, and Lydia stared at Beatrice and then at one another.

"But Cynthia's the best math student in the class," Sarah said, breaking the silence.

"Oh, no, she's not!" Beatrice basked in her new importance. "She just pretends to be. I heard her parents talking about her bad grades. She's going to have a tutor."

Lydia grew thoughtful. "Tell you what, Beatrice. Since you've been such a help, we are going to appoint you to a very big position in Alice's campaign. But you have to keep it a secret. You will be Liaison Spokesgirl of the Official Campaign of Alice for President. L-S-O-C-A-P—pronounced *SO*CAP. The *L* will have to be silent. Your job is to keep us informed about any fifth grader who has a sister in the first grade."

"What's 'liaison'?" Beatrice asked.

"It means you make a connection between things," Lydia explained. "You will keep us informed about certain Turnips by your connections with their little sisters."

"I see." Beatrice beamed. She felt very important.

The door bell rang. "I bet that's Hilary," Alice said.

Mrs. Whipple let Hilary in and told her the girls were in Alice's room.

"Well, it's about time!" Lydia frowned as Hilary rushed in.

Hilary was flushed and a little out of breath. "You'll never guess why I'm late." Hilary sat down on Alice's bed. "My mother had to drop me off in a taxi, or I wouldn't have made it at all." Hilary ran her fingers through her straight brown hair.

"This is a campaign strategy session for the election of the president of the fifth grade." Alice thought Hilary needed to be reminded of the seriousness of their endeavor.

"I had to buy a new pair of riding boots. They're English. Do you like them?" Hilary stretched out her legs and patted the boots. "Real leather. I just had my picture taken in Central Park on my horse. It's his birthday today." Hilary wiped a tiny speck off her boots.

Sarah groaned, and Alice nudged her. Alice knew that Sarah did not like Hilary.

"So?" Hilary looked up. "What's my job? I'd like to be CIA chief."

"You can't," said Lydia. "I'm the intelligence chief."

"I'd be better at it. I have a telephone in my bedroom, so I could make private calls. *And* I have a new tape recorder, which is very small, so it's good for taping secret conversations."

"Too bad," Lydia insisted. "Besides, if you're going to be late all the time—"

Alice had to think fast. She didn't want any conflicts. But Alice had to admit that Hilary was a snob and therefore bad for the political image of the Peaches.

"Tell you what," Alice interrupted. "I'd like Hilary to have an important *int*ernal job."

Hilary stared at Alice.

Alice continued. "I need a speech adviser, and since Hilary has a new tape recorder, she could help me practice my speech. She could even tape it for me and play it back so I can listen to myself."

Hilary said nothing.

"*And,*" Alice went on, "you'd have a very big title. You'd be Speech Adviser and General Co-ordinator of Alice's Campaign Committee."

"SAGCACC," declared Lydia.

"It's a bit hard to pronounce," Hilary pointed out.

"Yes, I guess it is," Alice conceded. "How

about SAG-COA-CAM-COM? That way it sounds
like a secret code."

"Hmmmm." Hilary sounded *almost* satis-
fied.

"It really is impressive, Hilary," Alice added.
"No one else has such a long title."

"Okay," said Hilary after a pause.

Alice wasn't sure that Hilary was convinced,
but she wanted to get on with the meeting. "And
now that that's settled," Alice said, turning to
Sarah, "what information do you have for us?"

"As you know," Sarah began, "in every election campaign there are polls."

Alice nodded. She knew about polls from
watching the seven o'clock news with her parents. Whenever there was an election, the news-
caster announced who was ahead in the latest
poll.

"I happen to know about polls," Sarah continued. "My father uses them to find out how
many people like his products." Sarah's father
was an advertising executive. "In fact, it's the
same with politics. My father says he can create
an image for a politician the same way he can for
dishwashing liquid."

Alice had heard that, too, but she remembered her parents saying you couldn't always
count on the polls. And her grandfather liked to
tell about the time the polls said Dewey would be
president of the United States, but Truman won
the election instead. You couldn't be too careful,
Alice reminded herself. Still, polls were useful,

and she was glad that Sarah was in charge of the polling for her campaign.

Sarah laid out three pages of names on Alice's desk.

TEN PEACHES	TEN TURNIPS	FIVE UNDECIDEDS
Alice	Donna	Susan
Sarah	Jane	Marcia
Lydia	Samantha	Claudine
Hilary	Tracey	Tania
Wing Chu	Jennifer	Dana
Wendy	Nina	
Marina	Kathy	
Toni	Cynthia	
Elizabeth	Sandra	
Caroline	Ellen	

"As you can see," Sarah explained, "there are twenty-five girls in our class. We need at least thirteen votes to elect Alice. There are ten Peaches—nine with the Defector." Sarah meant Marina. There are also ten Turnips. I decided to call everyone else an Undecided. I figure we need to get at least four votes from the Turnips or Un-decideds. And if we get Marina back, we'll have a margin of two votes, which will put us in a better position. Today is Monday," Sarah concluded. "We have until the end of this week to get votes. The election is one week from today."

Alice, Lydia, and Hilary studied the lists.

"Maybe," Alice said slowly, "the Peaches have been too exclusive. Maybe we will have to broaden our base."

"We don't want to broaden it too much," said Hilary. "The Peaches are a very select group."

"Listen, Hilary," Sarah said, sounding annoyed. "In order to win an election, you need as many votes as possible. You can't afford to be a snob." Sarah turned to Alice before Hilary had a chance to reply. "We'll need campaign posters," she said.

"Okay, Sarah. I'll work on some posters after I finish my homework tonight. My father can Xerox them tomorrow at his office."

"Good thinking, Alice." Sarah was pleased with the way the campaign was shaping up. "And," Sarah continued, "we will have to appeal to special interest groups."

"I have a plan to attract one of the Turnips," said Lydia.

"Who?"

"Kathy."

"How are you going to get her?" Alice wanted to know.

"Top secret," Lydia said and smiled mysteriously.

Alice knew that Lydia wasn't going to reveal her strategy.

"I'll think about appealing to the Undecideds," said Sarah.

"In that case," Lydia said, "we'll call you— wait a minute—it's coming to me." Lydia paused dramatically and gazed at the ceiling. "CUSIG! You'll be CUSIG! It has a mysterious ring to it, don't you think? Sort of Russian sounding." Lydia's favorite movie was *From Russia with Love.* She had seen all the James Bond movies.

"What is it?" Sarah asked.

"Coordinator for Undecided Special Interest Groups."

"Oh."

"And if it's boys Marina likes," said Alice, "I think I know how to get her!"

CHAPTER TWO

Alice Deals with the Defector

"Daddy!" Alice intercepted her father the next morning as he was racing toward the front door. He was half in and half out of his coat, groping frantically with his right arm for the missing sleeve.

Mr. Whipple worked in a bank on Wall Street. Every Tuesday he had an early-morning meeting.

"Here, let me help." Alice held her father's coat for him.

"Thanks, Alice. I can't talk now. I'm late for the office."

"It's just this." Alice handed her father a manila envelope filled with papers. "Will you make copies of these for me?"

Alice knew that her father's bank had a brand-new Xerox machine that made nice clean copies.

"What's in here?" he asked.

"Campaign posters."

"What?"

15

"You know, for class president. I'll need twenty-five copies of each one. Thanks a lot."

Before Mr. Whipple could reply, Alice thrust the envelope into his hands and ran down the hall.

"Beatrice!" she yelled. "Hurry up! We're late!"

Mr. Whipple shrugged, put Alice's envelope in his briefcase, and continued out the door.

"Come on, Beatrice. We'll miss the bus if you don't walk faster," Alice said, as they walked to the corner of Eighty-eighth Street and Park Avenue. Beatrice was trailing her Hello Kitty book bag on the pavement. Every few moments she would give it a jerk and mutter something under her breath.

"You don't need that silly book bag. Everyone knows first graders don't have homework. It's not as if you need a whole bag for your jacks."

"It's not a book bag," insisted Beatrice. "It's Spot. And I can't go any faster because he likes to stop and sniff. Come on, Spot." Beatrice tugged at the bag. She was not allowed to have a real dog because the pediatrician had advised against it. Beatrice was allergic to animal fur.

"Well, you'd better move. The bus is turning the corner." Alice grabbed Beatrice's hand and ran up the street to the bus stop, dragging Beatrice and her book bag behind.

Miss Barton's School was about as far east in Manhattan as you could get. It was located on

Eighty-first Street at the end of a cul-de-sac that overlooked the East River. The school bus started at Ninety-sixth Street and Park Avenue and went down to Seventy-ninth, where it turned and went crosstown to Eighty-first Street and East End.

"That was close," Alice gasped as the bus doors closed. "Maybe next time you can leave Spot at home. Dogs aren't allowed in school, anyway." She and Beatrice started down the aisle looking for seats.

"Hi, Alice. Hi, Beatrice."

"Hi, Toni. Hi, Caroline." Alice turned to Beatrice. "You sit over there." Alice pointed to an empty seat close to the front. She saw Marina sitting alone all the way at the back. "I have something important to attend to."

"But that's not fair. You promised to sit with me and help me with my spelling."

Even though Miss Barton's didn't start homework officially until the fourth grade, the younger girls were given weekly spelling lists to memorize and lots of math facts.

"Listen, Beatrice." Alice spoke softly, but it was clear that she had made up her mind. "Do what I say. I'll explain later."

"Promise?"

"Promise."

Alice edged her way down the aisle and sat down beside Marina.

"Hello, Marina." Alice looked depressed.

"What's the matter, Alice? Why are you whispering?" Marina whispered, too.

Alice leaned closer to Marina's ear. "I'm glad you're sitting by yourself. I have some disturbing news." Alice paused. "It's a crisis!"

"A what? I can't hear you, Alice," whispered Marina.

"A *crisis!*" bellowed Alice. Every head in the bus turned toward her and Marina. Alice ignored the stares and went on in a whisper. "A crisis that affects each and every Peach. A crisis of *loyalty*. A crisis of *honor*. A crisis of *truth*." Alice paused to let the words sink in.

Marina looked nervous. Her eyes darted back and forth. She twisted her hands in her lap.

Definite signs of guilt, thought Alice as she considered what to say next. "It has come to my attention," she continued gravely, "that there has been a d-e-f-e-c-t-i-o-n." Alice spelled the last word. "One of our fellow Peaches has defected to the Turnip enemy!" Alice stopped once again to let Marina absorb the seriousness of her message.

"I haven't heard anything like that," said Marina. "Who told you, Alice?" Marina squirmed in her seat and twirled a strand of her long, brown hair around her finger.

"I have my sources," said Alice loftily. "The question is, who is it? That's why I wanted to speak to you first. I know that I can count on your loyalty. You, of all Peaches, know how important it is that a Peach attain the highest office in the class. I know that I can depend on you to help me in this, our gravest hour." Alice stared into Marina's eyes.

"Of—of course, Alice. Of course you can count on me." Marina looked down and pretended she was straightening out the wrinkles in her uniform skirt.

"Good," said Alice. "Look at Beatrice," she continued, changing the subject and talking in a normal voice. "Look how she's sitting there pouting just because I told her I wanted to sit with you. It's so boring to have a little sister. If I could choose, I'd like an older brother. Wouldn't you, Marina? Like Donna has."

Marina looked up.

"Brothers are so much more useful than sisters," Alice persisted. "For example, if you need someone to go to the square dance with, a brother always has a friend. Oh, well, I guess I'm pretty lucky. My friend Peter lives across the street. He's practically like an older brother. He's always coming over to our apartment." Alice couldn't help noticing how interested Marina was in what she was saying. "Peter's *tall,* and he's in the *sixth* grade. It's too bad I already have someone to go to the square dance with, or I'd invite him.

"Well, here we are at school. See you in class, Marina." Alice jumped up and started for the front of the bus. She stopped suddenly and turned back toward Marina. "Maybe you'd like to come over some afternoon after school?"

"Oh, gee, Alice. I'd love to."

Maybe she *had* exaggerated a bit, thought Alice to herself as she hopped off the bus. Peter wasn't exactly tall *now,* but her mother always said he would be someday because he took after his father. And even if Peter wasn't exactly in the sixth grade, he *had* been put into sixth-grade math.

The important thing was that it had worked. She would just have to make sure that Marina didn't actually meet Peter until *after* the election.

CHAPTER THREE

A Lesson in American History

"Okay, troops, today we recruit one Turnip and one Undecided." Alice met Sarah and Lydia on the way to homeroom, the first class of the day. "Lydia, you said you had a plan to attract Kathy to our side. And, Sarah, I'm counting on you to deal with at least one Undecided. I've already started working on the Defector. Report back to me at lunch."

The eight o'clock bell rang. Alice, Sarah, and Lydia hurried to class.

"*Good* morning, girls," Mrs. Parker greeted her homeroom class. Mrs. Parker was a cheerful, slightly plump lady with short, blond hair. To Alice she always looked as if she were smiling because she had such large teeth and wide, round eyeglasses. Alice liked the way Mrs. Parker bounced on her bright green Nike running shoes.

After taking attendance and making announcements, Mrs. Parker began the history lesson. "Today we will review some principles of self-government. As you know, our election for

21

class president will take place next Monday. You will be voting between two very worthy candidates, Alice Whipple and Donna Ellington."

"In America we have a two-party system, the Democrats and Republicans. In our class elections we have two candidates but not two parties."

Alice thought it was a good thing Mrs. Parker didn't know that the class practically did have a two-party system, the Peaches and the Turnips. Cliques were not encouraged at Miss Barton's.

Wing Chu raised her hand. "Do all Americans have to be Republicans or Democrats?"

"No. Not exactly. Most of them are, though. The others are called Independents," Mrs. Parker replied.

"Psssst," whispered Lydia, nudging Alice. "She means the Undecideds."

Mrs. Parker continued. "Each candidate has a *slate*, which means a running mate who will become vice-president. After our class elections, the president will choose her own secretary-treasurer. We will vote by secret ballot just as we do in the national election. In this country only native-born Americans have the right to run for president, but every adult American citizen, wherever he or she may have come from originally, is entitled to vote. That is why our government is called a democracy, a term that comes from ancient Greek and means 'the people rule.'"

Jane's hand went up. "Girls didn't used to be able to vote," she pointed out.

"No, that's true," agreed Mrs. Parker. "Does anyone remember the name of the women who fought for the right to vote?"

"I do." Donna looked up brightly. "Suffragettes. They used to demonstrate and march. They even chained themselves to lamp posts and went to jail."

"Very good, Donna. That's right."

Alice raised her hand. "How come there has never been a *girl* president?" Alice glanced at Marina and was glad to see her blush. *Serves her right,* Alice thought. She thinks boys are so great. Alice was also pleased that Marina had three new pimples on her chin.

"That's hard to say," Mrs. Parker replied. "But there's no reason why there couldn't be one. There have been women leaders in other countries, for example, in India and England. Maybe by the time you are grown-up, we will have a woman in the White House."

Marina spoke up. "What would happen to the first lady if a girl was president?"

"That's easy, silly," Sarah said. "We'd have to have a Mrs. President and a first man."

The class giggled.

Lydia took advantage of the distraction to hand Kathy, a Turnip, a note under the desk. Lydia was about to execute her plan to attract Kathy to Alice's side in the election. Kathy kept the note on her lap while she read it so Mrs. Parker wouldn't notice. It said, "Top Secret: Meet me in the fourth-floor broom closet at recess. Solution to milk problem at hand!"

Hilary still had her mind on the first lady. "But if there's a first man," she asked, "who would be the hostess and run the parties?"

What a snob, thought Alice. *Just because her parents were invited to dinner at the White House last year, she thinks she's so great.*

"Oh, my dear, I wouldn't worry about that," said Mrs. Parker. "I'm sure they would think of something. And now, girls, I would like to continue with our review." Mrs. Parker smiled. "Each candidate needs a *platform*. That means she and her assistants, called *aides* in a real election, choose a point of view and make *proposals*. Proposals are suggestions for ways of doing things or new ideas that might help the country. If the voters like the proposals, they choose the candidate on that basis."

Lydia waved her hand. Her ponytail flopped back and forth.

"Yes, Lydia?"

"What about the secret service, and security, and body guards, and wire tapping, and bribery—"

"Wire tapping and bribery are illegal, Lydia. In America voters have to make up their own minds. Politicians are not allowed to buy votes. Each candidate has to convince the voters that he or she is the best choice for the job."

Alice's hand went up again. "Does that mean we can make campaign posters with slogans on them like the ones you see on lampposts and mailboxes for real elections?"

"Why, Alice, what a good idea. I hadn't even thought of that. Both you and Donna could sketch some out at home and then color them in during an art class."

Alice was pleased with herself. At least she had a head start there. She had already begun her campaign posters.

"But remember," Mrs. Parker said, looking at the clock and seeing that it was nearly the end of the period, "this is a *democratic system*. The election must be run fairly, without bullying or coercion—"

"Pssssst, Alice," Lydia whispered. "I don't think Mrs. Parker knows very much about real elections."

"And," Mrs. Parker was still talking, "the *electorate*, which means the voters, must vote according to the candidate's platform and good character, not just for their best friends. I know we are all looking forward to the election speeches, which Alice and Donna will make to the class on Friday."

Just as Mrs. Parker pronounced "Friday," the bell rang. The girls grabbed their science books and thundered from the room.

CHAPTER FOUR

Measuring Mealworms

Alice's best friend Sarah entered the science room and sat at the back next to Dana. Dana was one of the shortest girls in the class. Sarah thought she was babyish because she wore braids and cried easily. Sarah decided that it would be easy to persuade Dana to vote for Alice.

"Good morning, girls," Mr. Moffet, the fifth-grade science teacher, said as he loped into the classroom. He looked like a string bean, Sarah thought. He was definitely weird. He wasn't like other teachers at Miss Barton's. He wore a gold earring in his left ear and played the bass in a jazz club on weekends. And even though he was strict, he liked to make jokes.

"Today we are going to *bend* our thoughts to the lowly mealworm." Mr. Moffet pronounced "bend" very slowly and sort of curved himself forward as he said it. "Although mealworms are small creatures—as you shall soon see since part of your task will be to measure them—"

"Yuck," said Jennifer. "Who wants to measure worms!"

26

"Yuck?" said Mr. Moffet. "Are you expressing an opinion, Jennifer, or merely venting an emotion? In either case, perhaps you could wait until after you have done the work."

"Yes, Mr. Moffet."

"As I was saying, the mealworm is a small creature, but in the course of its short life it goes through profound changes. It begins life as a small, white blob and continues through its 'grub' or 'larva' stage as a mealworm." Mr. Moffet wrote out the words *larva* and *grub* on the blackboard. While his back was turned, Sarah tapped Dana on the shoulder.

"Pssst! Dana!"

Dana turned around. "What is it, Sarah?" she whispered.

"Who are you voting for?"

"Well, I haven't—"

"But surely, Alice is the best candidate."

"Sarah!" Mr. Moffet's voice boomed. He was still writing on the board. "Perhaps you would like to share your thoughts with the rest of us." Mr. Moffet spun around and stared at the two girls. "I assume you and Dana were discussing mealworms."

"Not exactly," mumbled Sarah, turning red.

"Well, then, *I* was. Although the mealworm starts off as a small blob, it quickly turns into an actual worm. This is the form you will be studying today. As you will see, the mealworm is tan and possesses a hard outer skeleton. I want each of you to take a specimen from here," Mr. Moffet said as he tapped the shoe box on his desk. "And I want you to place it on one of these metal trays." He pointed to the aluminum trays stacked in a pile beside the shoe box. "You will begin by measuring your mealworm. Then you will draw and label it in your notebooks."

Sarah and Dana were the last in the line for the mealworms and the last back to their desks. Sarah kept hoping that Mr. Moffet would stop talking long enough for her to speak to Dana, but he went on to describe how mealworms turned into beetles. Sarah thought it was interesting that one thing could have so many different shapes, but all the same, she found it hard to concentrate. She kept wondering how she could persuade Dana to vote for Alice.

When all the girls had returned to their desks, Mr. Moffet told them to begin.

It was then that the trouble started. How were they to measure something that wiggled, even if mealworms wiggled less than most worms? Sarah managed by jamming her mealworm against the edge of her ruler and holding it in place. She figured it couldn't hurt it because of its shell. But Dana wasn't so lucky. Sarah looked up from her tray just in time to see Dana's tray tip over and her mealworm fall to the floor. Dana disappeared under her desk in search of the specimen.

Sarah dived under the desk after Dana.

"Oh, Sarah, thanks. Will you pick it up? I don't want to touch it!"

"You don't? How can you measure it if you don't touch it?"

"Well, I thought maybe you might measure it for me."

"I *might* be able to, if Mr. Moffet wasn't looking."

"Gosh, thanks, Sarah."

"I'd need you to do me a favor, though."

"Anything."

"I'd like to think you *want* to vote for Alice."

"But I sort of promised Donna. . . ."

"What does 'sort of' mean?"

"Well, Donna said my vote was important to her. She has some really good ideas—"

"Do you, or do you not, want me to pick up and measure your mealworm?"

"Of course I do. But Donna wants to—"

"And when we're finished with mealworms, we'll probably do something really disgusting and slimy like *leeches*. Leeches belong to the same family as mealworms. And they suck your blood when you touch them. Like in *The African Queen*, where Humphrey Bogart has to go under water to fix the boat and there were trillions of leeches all over him. Katharine Hepburn had to pull them off. She had to pull hard, too, because they really stick."

"That's awful! Would you do my mealworm *and* my leeches?"

"And Alice?"

"Well—"

"No Alice, no mealworm and no leeches."

"All right," Dana agreed. She looked up and banged her head on the desk. There was a giggle in the classroom. Sarah and Dana crawled out from under the desk as fast as they could. All of a sudden they were staring down at the soft brown suede of Mr. Moffet's shoes.

"You'll find the missing mealworm over to the left, ladies. I don't think both of you are required to retrieve it, do you?"

Sarah blushed. She picked up the worm and returned it to Dana's tray. Being a campaign manager was turning out to be a lot harder than Sarah had originally thought.

It was recess and although Lydia had been in the fourth-floor broom closet for only three minutes, it felt like hours. She sat in the dark on an upside-down water bucket, wondering if Kathy would come. The whole closet shook as the girls ran down the hall toward the staircase. They would be on their way outside, Lydia told herself.

It's awfully hot in here, Lydia thought. She felt a drop of perspiration run down her cheek. *And it sure is spooky. Still, I have to put up with discomfort if I want to be a good undercover agent. James Bond wouldn't complain.*

Lydia leaned back and rested against the wall. Suddenly she froze. Something moved on top of her head. It was soft. *Oh, no! It's moving! It must be alive!* It felt the littlest bit wet, too. Lydia remembered with horror the scene in which the spider crawled across James Bond's chest as he lay helpless in bed.

Two knocks at the door startled Lydia so much that she jumped and turned on the light. Her head hit against a mop, and she realized that one of its strands had been tickling her hair. The bucket clattered against the wall.

Lydia opened the door. "Quick!" she said to Kathy. "Come inside before someone sees you." She turned off the light again and closed the door.

"What's going on, Lydia? And why are we in the dark?"

"You can't be too careful," replied Lydia. "Someone might be listening."

"But the hall's empty. Everyone's gone outside or is in the classroom having milk and fruit. Milk, yuck!"

"Exactly," said Lydia. "That's what I wanted to talk to you about. We have to make sure that no one knows we're here, and our conversation has to remain a secret."

"Oh."

"I called you here today," Lydia began, "to discuss a matter of grave consequence to the entire fifth grade." Lydia's parents always discussed matters of grave consequence when they expected her to listen to them.

"Oh?"

"Yes. As you know, there is a presidential election next week. Alice has singled you out as a

Special Interest Group." Lydia paused, hoping
Kathy was impressed.

"Oh? It's funny in here with no lights."

She doesn't sound impressed, Lydia thought.
"Yes," Lydia went on. "A *very* special interest
group. It has to do with milk."

"Oh?"

That's better, thought Lydia. A sign of interest at last.

"Alice is very sensitive to your feelings
about milk. And so are the rest of the Peaches. In
fact, Alice needs your vote in order to be elected
class president." There, she'd said it.

"Oh. Well—" Kathy hesitated—"I *was* going
to vote for Donna."

"We thought you'd change your mind when
we told you about the milk. You see, Alice and
Sarah and I have agreed that we will drink your
milk every day at lunch for a month when the
teachers aren't looking."

Kathy hated milk, and Miss Barton's had a
rule that up to the sixth grade girls had to drink
at least one small glass of milk at lunch. A few
weeks earlier Kathy had been sent to the headmistress's office for pouring hers into the flower
arrangement on the table.

"Would you really? I mean really?"

Well, finally! Lydia heaved a sigh of relief.
Being a politician certainly wasn't easy. "You'd
have to vote for Alice, of course. Politics works
that way. We do something for you, and you help
us in return."

"That would be disloyal to Donna and Jane. But—"

"Yes?"

"Well—maybe—if you drank my milk for *two* months."

"I think I could persuade Alice and Sarah to agree to six weeks. *And*—when Alice is president, she will lobby to have the milk rule changed to fruit juice."

"Okay. It's a deal. Starting today, you drink my milk."

"Deal."

"Shake."

The bell rang, signaling the end of recess. Kathy and Lydia rushed from the broom closet to their next class.

"There's no need to shout, Gerald." Mrs. Whipple held the phone away from her ear. "I can hear perfectly well."

It was three o'clock. Alice and Beatrice had not gotten home yet.

"It's downright embarrassing. I gave my secretary a stack of papers to Xerox, and she came back twittering. What are they teaching them in that school, anyway? It's *your* fault, Mary. *You* insisted on sending them there. The best school in New York, you said."

"It's self-government, dear. I'm sure if you calm down, you'll understand. Alice is running for class president. She made some campaign posters."

"Mary, have you actually *seen* what she made?"

"No-o-o-o." Mrs. Whipple remembered the year before when Alice had decided to become an inventor. It had taken hours to clean up the sticky chocolate furniture polish that Alice had spread over the dining room table.

"Mary, are you there?"

"Yes, dear." Mrs. Whipple was still thinking about Alice's invention.

"I pay good money to send them to that school."

"Yes, dear. Of course you do. I'm sure there's a perfectly good explanation. We'll talk to Alice tonight when you get home."

"You bet we will!"

As Alice and Sarah were waiting to get on the school bus, Lydia raced by.

"Beware, a Turnip!" she whispered, speeding past.

Alice and Sarah looked quickly over their shoulders. Sure enough, there was Jane. But she was at the other end of the block.

"Don't you think Lydia is overdoing it a bit?" asked Sarah. "I mean, I know we have to be careful, but—"

Lydia raced by again, this time coming from the opposite direction.

"Mission in broom closet accomplished," she panted.

"Calm down, Lydia," Alice said, grabbing Lydia's school blazer.

"But, Alice, we shouldn't be seen together. You know, security."

"Okay, Lydia. This will only take a minute. The progress report for now is: one Undecided from Sarah, a Turnip from you, and the Defector from me." Alice smiled. "That means only two more to go. And after what Beatrice told us about Cynthia, I think we can convince her to vote for Sarah and me."

Alice let go of Lydia's blazer and watched her disappear around the corner.

"Hi, Marina." Alice waved as Marina started crossing to the other side of the street. *Obviously avoiding us,* Alice thought. *Her conscience is still bothering her.*

"Aren't you coming on the bus?" The light turned red, and Marina had to wait.

"No. Can't. I'm late for my dance lesson."

Alice had her now. "That reminds me. Peter's a great dancer. He's been taking dance lessons for *three* years."

"Well, Donna said her brother might take me to the square dance if he's here that weekend." The light changed to green, and Marina crossed.

"Peter doesn't have a rash on his neck," Alice called after her.

"What was that all about?" Sarah wanted to know.

"Nothing much. Just working on a Special Interest Group. I think the Defector will have to be watched."

CHAPTER FIVE

The Campaign Continues

That afternoon Alice was in her room by supposedly doing her homework. Instead, she was planning her speech. She looked at Sarah's election lists and tried to devise strategies to attract Special Interest Groups. At the moment she was concentrating on Claudine, the student from France. Claudine was an Undecided.

Maybe if Alice promised Claudine to lobby for Brie and croissants instead of cream cheese and raisin bread at lunch—

A sharp knock on her door interrupted Alice's train of thought. "Alice, your father wants to see you," said Mrs. Whipple, poking her head around the door. "I think you'd better come quickly."

"Oh, good. He must have my campaign posters. I'll be right there." Alice gathered up the lists and put them back in the file marked "Campaign Strategy. Top Secret. Beware." She slipped the file into the top drawer of her desk. As she stepped out of her room, she bumped into Beatrice.

"Okay, Miss Busybody. Now you can see my campaign posters."

Mr. Whipple stood beside the dining room table with his arms crossed. Alice thought he looked a bit stiff, like an Egyptian statue. Except that Egyptian statues didn't tap their feet. Then she saw the Xeroxes spread out on the table.

"Oh, thanks, Daddy. They look wonderful. Just wait until I color them in."

"Alice! They do *not* look wonderful. They are a disgrace." Mr. Whipple uncrossed his arms and pointed at the display. "You cannot take these to school."

"But those are my campaign posters!"

"Has your teacher seen these?"

"No. But she said it was okay for us to make posters and write slogans. She said it was a great idea. And I was the one who thought of it."

"Then I suggest you redo them. These slogans are libelous, Alice. Just listen to this." Mr. Whipple read them aloud.

"Only Dimwits Vote for Donna.

A Is for Alice
D Is for Donna
Up in the Air with Alice
Down in the Dumps with Donna.

Bookworms Make Bad Presidents.

Plain Jane Is a Big Pain."

Mr. Whipple stopped reading and glared at Alice.

"But, Daddy, what's wrong with them? They're just like the campaign ads on TV."

"Alice, this is not TV. This is an election at Miss Barton's School. You are going to be in the same class with Donna and her friends for eight years. You can't run your campaign on insults. You need good reasons why you think you would make a better class president than Donna. Instead of criticizing Donna and Jane, you should think about what you can do for the class."

"But Donna *is* a bookworm!"

"So was Thomas Jefferson, and he was a great president."

"And Jane *is* plain. She has practically no chin, and she wears glasses with *wire* frames."

"Alice!" Mr. Whipple's tone was decidedly sharp. "Looks have nothing to do with being a good person. Besides, if you would bother to look through some history books at pictures of our best presidents, you would see that they were not all handsome."

"But it's important for their wives to be pretty," Alice pointed out.

"Eleanor Roosevelt wasn't pretty," Mrs. Whipple said. "She was one of America's greatest first ladies."

"Oh." Alice grew thoughtful.

"And look at Miss Partridge," observed Beatrice. Miss Partridge was headmistress of Miss Barton's. "*She* doesn't have a chin, either."

"You mean," said Alice slowly, "I shouldn't criticize Donna. I should make people *want* to vote for me?"

"Exactly." Mr. Whipple heaved a sigh of relief.

Alice realized her father was right. She would have to make people *want* to vote for her. It was no good just being negative about Donna and Jane. She had to be positive about herself.

Alice decided to change her campaign strategy. There was no better place to start than with Cynthia. She knew that Cynthia would *want* to vote for her after their conversation.

Mr. and Mrs. Whipple were talking in the living room.

Beatrice was in the kitchen rearranging the magnetic letters on the refrigerator.

Alice walked quietly down the hall into the study. She didn't want to disturb anyone, and she wanted her conversation with Cynthia to be private.

Alice dialed Cynthia's number.

"Hello, may I please speak to Cynthia?" Alice was thinking her most positive thoughts. "Hello, Cynthia. This is Alice. I'm polling the class. When I'm president, I want to do the best I can for everyone." Alice felt she was being very positive.

"Who says you're going to be president?"

Alice suddenly felt a little less positive, but she pressed on. "As a matter of fact, Cynthia, that's just what I'm calling about. I think I'm in a position to help you."

"Not as much as Donna. She promised to make me secretary-treasurer."

"I have something better than that, Cynthia."

"Like what?"

Alice took a deep breath and tried to sound casual. "I don't think it's fair for people to talk about other people's grades. Do you, Cynthia?"

Alice could hear Cynthia breathing. She went on. "Of course it's okay if you want to tell somebody your *own* grade, but I don't think it's very nice talking about *other* people's grades. Especially if they're *bad*." Alice lingered on her last word before continuing. "For example, if somebody got a bad grade on a test—like a math test— and then pretended she did very well, and if it turned out that she needed a math tutor, when everybody thought she was the best in the class, well, I think it's that person's own business, don't you? But *some* people like going around talking about it."

"Who's going around talking, Alice?"

"Oh, people."

"How many people?"

"A few people."

"How much are they talking, Alice?"

"Not too much—yet." Alice paused. "Of course, I could probably make them stop. Especially if I get elected president."

"Do you really think you could?"

"Yes, Cynthia. *If* I'm elected president."

Mr. Whipple entered the study. "Here you are, Alice," her father said. "Your mother sent me to find you. Dinner's ready."

"Oh. Hi, Daddy." Alice turned to her father and then back to the phone. "I've got to go now, Cynthia. I'll see you at school tomorrow." Alice replaced the receiver.

"Thank you so much for your advice, Daddy," Alice said, beaming. "I followed it and it worked perfectly. Gosh, I'm hungry. Campaigning really makes you hungry. I'll work on my speech after dinner."

Later that same evening Hilary called. "Hi, Alice. You'll never guess where I am. I'm in the garage downstairs in our building on the floor of my father's Mercedes. He just had a telephone installed last week. It's great for long trips, especially when you get stuck on the Long Island Expressway."

Oh, gosh, not again, Alice thought. Aloud she said, "Why don't you call from your house?"

"That's not exciting, Alice. I had to sneak down here with the car keys. It's much more secret. Listen, Alice, I've been thinking—"

"Yes?"

"Well, I thought it would be really nice if you promised to appoint me secretary-treasurer."

"Listen, Hilary. I can't. I have to keep it for Turnips and Undecideds. The post of secretary-treasurer is very important, and I'm saving it for a special occasion."

Alice hoped Hilary understood.

"Oh—" Hilary paused. "Well, okay, Alice, if that's the way you want it. But I *would* like to be secretary-treasurer, anyway. I just thought you ought to know. Well, bye."

"By the way, Hilary—"

"Yes?"

"There *is* something else you could do."

"What's that, Alice?"

"Well, you know how *awful* our recess snacks are?"

"What's that got to do with being secretary-treasurer?"

"Hilary, do you or do you not want to help me win votes?"

Hilary paused a moment. "Y-e-e-e-s," she said slowly.

"Well, I thought if we baked some brownies and distributed them at recess, we could win some votes for our side."

"But what has that got to do with *me*?"

"I thought that since you had such a big kitchen in your house that you might like to bake some brownies."

"Brownies! You want *me* to cook, Alice?"

"What's wrong with that? Politicians have to attract voters any way they can."

"I don't cook, Alice. In fact, our cook doesn't like us to come near the kitchen."

Alice was glad that Sarah hadn't heard Hilary's last remark. Sarah had to do the dishes every night, all by herself. Her brother was too young to do anything but fold the napkins. But even Sarah would agree that Hilary's vote was important.

"Wait a minute, Hilary. Don't forget that *after* the election, you'll be a member of my inner circle. That's like a high-level cabinet post in real government. And you'll be able to help make important decisions about life in the fifth grade—Hilary? Are you there?"

"Yes, I'm here, Alice. I was just thinking."

"Thinking? About what?"

"Oh, things. Well, I guess I'd better hang up."

"Okay, Hilary. See you at school tomorrow. We still have a lot of work to do. Bye."

"Bye, Alice."

Alice congratulated herself on her brilliant idea. If Hilary wouldn't make brownies, she would. But the brownie mix would cost money, and Alice didn't want to spend her own allowance on it.

CHAPTER SIX

Kitchen Politics

Alice had a flute lesson in the music room after school the next day so she went home a half hour late.

When Alice rushed into the apartment and dumped her book bag in the hall, Beatrice was already home.

"How was school, Alice?" Mrs. Whipple asked. "Ready for your snack?"

"Can't now, Mom. Going over to Peter's for a few minutes. Then Sarah's coming over."

"I'm coming with you," said Beatrice.

"No, you're not."

"I am, too. If you don't let me come, I'll tell Cynthia—"

"All right. But"— Alice peered straight down at Beatrice—"if you say one word about anything, I'll feed Salisbury to Sir Lancelot." Sir Lancelot was Peter's pet boa constrictor.

"Boas don't eat turtles, stupid."

"He'll eat this one."

* * *

"Why, hello, Alice. And Beatrice. What a nice surprise. We haven't seen you for a long time," said Mrs. Hildreth as she opened the door to her apartment.

"She must want something," said Peter, coming up behind his mother.

"Hi, Mrs. Hildreth." Alice pretended she hadn't heard Peter.

"Beatrice and I thought we'd drop in and see how Sir Lancelot is doing."

"Well, that's very nice. Come on in."

"Are you president yet?" Peter's younger brother James called from his bedroom.

"Not exactly. The campaign is still in progress." Alice turned to Beatrice. "Don't you want to play with James?"

"No. I want to see Sir Lancelot."

Alice and Beatrice followed Peter to his room.

Sir Lancelot dozed in his cage. Alice studied his scales. "We had to measure mealworms yesterday," she said. "They wiggle a lot more than he does. That reminds me, Peter."

"Yes?"

"Has anyone invited you to our class square dance yet?"

"The girls in your class are all too tall. They're stuck-up, too."

Alice knew that Peter was embarrassed about his size. He was one of the shortest boys in his class. "Marina's not too tall," she said. "And she's not at all stuck-up. You've never met her because she's new this year."

"But—" Beatrice began. Alice thumped her hard on the back. "Don't cough, Beatrice," she said. "It's bad for your tonsils. And," Alice said, lowering her voice, "remember Salisbury."

"She's probably fat and ugly," Peter said, thinking about Marina.

"Yeah," added James who had wandered in to join the others. "With three huge pimples on her nose. Girls always get pimples in the fifth grade."

Alice ignored James. "Marina has the lead in the middle school play this year. It's *Sleeping Beauty*," said Alice with emphasis on 'Beauty.'"

"Oh?"

Alice detected a flicker of interest in Peter's voice. She knew he'd played Pinocchio in his class play the last year. Peter was quite interested in acting.

"Does she want someone to go to the dance with?" Peter asked softly.

"I could ask her," Alice offered. "Maybe I could even arrange it. *If* you donated two weeks' allowance to my campaign fund."

"Why do you need money to be elected class president?" James asked.

"Every campaign has a fund. There are a lot of expenses in running for office," Alice said.

"How about one week's allowance?" Peter suggested.

"One and a half."

"Okay. It's a deal."

Alice looked at her watch. "Oh, gosh! I forgot the time! Sarah is coming over to work on the campaign for an hour before dinner. I've got to go. Come on, Beatrice."

As soon as Alice and Beatrice were out in the street, Beatrice tugged at Alice's sleeve. "I thought you said Wendy was Sleeping Beauty?" Beatrice said.

"She is. I said Marina was *in Sleeping Beauty*. I did not say she *was* Sleeping Beauty. And, anyway, the witch has the most important part."

After dinner that evening Alice and Beatrice began making brownies. Alice added walnuts, raisins, and chocolate chips to the Duncan Hines brownie mix. Peter's allowance had covered all the necessary expenses. Sarah was in Alice's room working on the campaign. Mr. and Mrs. Whipple were watching the evening news on the television in the study.

"If you insist on helping, Beatrice, you have to stir faster. And stop tasting the batter. There won't be enough. I need twenty-five brownies."

Beatrice made a face. "But it's not sweet enough. It needs more sugar."

"The sugar's already in the mix, stupid."

"Alice!" Sarah called. "I've finished. Come look." Sarah was coloring in Alice's new batch of campaign posters.

"Okay, I'll be right there. And don't you dare

take another taste, Beatrice. Just keep stirring. I'll be right back." Alice left the kitchen.

Beatrice stuck her finger in the batter again. It definitely needed sugar. Just because Alice had a little baby fat didn't mean the brownies should taste terrible and that everyone else had to go without sugar. Beatrice decided to add some. She reached for the sugar container and poured. *That should do it,* she thought. She mixed it in. The batter looked delicious. After looking around to make sure that Alice hadn't returned, Beatrice tasted it once more, just to make sure.

She had made a terrible mistake.

When the brownies had cooled, Alice and Sarah wrapped each one individually in Saran Wrap.

"Why are you putting labels on the brownies?" Beatrice asked.

"They're not labels. They're small campaign posters. Can't you read?"

Beatrice peered at one of the labels. Each one had a heart and a balloon drawn with marker. "Vote for Alice," Beatrice read out loud. "That's a funny thing to write on a brownie."

"Not if you want to be president of your class. Everyone likes brownies."

"Oh," said Beatrice. She was glad that Alice hadn't tasted *these* brownies.

CHAPTER SEVEN

A Blessing in Disguise

The bell rang for recess. Alice ran to her locker and dialed her combination. She was pleased with her timing. It was Thursday. The speeches were scheduled for the next day, Friday. The brownies would be a definite advantage.

Alice removed her book bag and ran back with it to the snack trolley in the fifth grade homeroom. That day was the perfect day for brownies. Everyone hated banana chips and dried prunes. Brownies would go much better with milk. Alice carefully arranged the brownies so that the "Vote for Alice" labels were facing up.

"Look, everybody!" Sarah shouted. "Alice has brought the class a treat."

"What is it?" asked Dana, who never ate her recess snack.

"I decided to bake brownies for the whole class. They'll give us energy for our math test next period."

"Brownies? That's bribery!" Donna was outraged.

"It is not. It's a special treat."

"Then how come you have 'Vote for Alice' labels on the brownies?"

"Those aren't labels. Those are small campaign posters. They just happen to fit on the brownies. Mrs. Parker said we were allowed to make campaign posters, remember?"

Donna was not convinced. But she couldn't resist a brownie.

Before Alice had a chance to unwrap her brownie, three of the girls were clutching their throats and gagging.

"I've been poisoned," gasped Jane.

"So have I!" Kathy said.

"Me, too," groaned Cynthia. "I'm much too sick to take the math test."

"Who is sick?" demanded Mrs. Parker. "What is going on here?"

"Alice gave us poison brownies," said Donna.

"What is the meaning of this, Alice?" Mrs. Parker looked sternly at Alice.

"I don't understand," Alice said. "Beatrice, my sister, and I baked brownies for the whole class last night. Something must have happened to them." Alice decided she'd better taste the brownies herself and see what the trouble was. She took a tiny bite. "Somebody messed up my brownies! They taste like salt!"

"Sabotage!" Lydia shouted. "I told you not to trust anybody!"

"When I went to England last summer, three people got food poisoning from eating on the plane," Hilary announced, clutching her stomach and doubling over.

"It could be serious," Alice said slowly. She realized that there was a way to turn this disaster to her advantage. "I made those brownies from a Duncan Hines brownie mix. Someone must have tampered with them! Anything might be in them. I think we should all be checked by the nurse."

Math period was almost over by the time Mrs. Tully, the school nurse, had finished checking all twenty-five fifth graders. It was much too late for them to take the math test. Mrs. Tully had been very sympathetic, but in her view there was nothing seriously wrong with the brownies. Someone had added salt.

Alice knew who that someone was. It was not the first time that Beatrice had mistaken the salt for the sugar. But it was definitely the last time Alice would let her stir. When she thought about it, though, Alice had to admit that things had turned out quite well. Everyone in the class agreed that it was worth a mouthful of salt to miss the math test.

CHAPTER EIGHT

Speech Day

The Friday for the election speeches finally arrived. They were to be given during history period. Alice was feeling nervous. She had worked on her speech most of Thursday evening. Sarah and Lydia had helped, and Hilary had let her use her tape recorder. But Alice was, after all, responsible.

Mrs. Parker had borrowed the lectern from the school auditorium. It stood at the front of the classroom facing the rows of desks. The walls were decorated with campaign posters. Alice found them boring. Her father had made her take out all the good slogans. "Vote for Alice" was definitely dull. At least Donna's weren't any better.

When the bell rang, Mrs. Parker rapped her desk with a ruler and called for quiet.

"As you know, girls, today we will be hearing Donna and Alice present their platforms for class president. I want all of you to listen carefully. In a democratic election it is essential to know exactly what each candidate stands for so that you can vote intelligently. Donna will speak first."

Alice was glad that Donna had asked to be the first speaker. She watched Donna get up from her desk and walk slowly to the front of the class. Donna spread her speech out on the lectern, cleared her throat, and began. Alice thought she looked very self-assured. She wore barrettes with ribbons down to her shoulders.

"Friends and fellow classmates—"

Gosh, Alice thought, *she sounds awfully professional!*

"Now that we are in fifth grade, we are allowed to elect class officers. Mrs. Parker has helped a lot by explaining the election process to us," Donna continued and smiled at her teacher.

Goody-goody, thought Alice.

"What I want to say first," Donna proceeded, "is that it doesn't matter who wins the election, what does count is our school spirit and our class spirit. We must all work together to keep Miss Barton's as good as it is and to make it even better."

"Bravo!" Mrs. Parker cheered Donna on.

"Thank you, Mrs. Parker."

Teacher's pet, thought Alice.

Donna went on. "If you elect me president, I promise to treat everybody fairly, and I promise to listen to all your suggestions and ideas.

"For our class project I think we should collect all our old toys. We could fix them up and then give them to children who need them. I also think that we should start a class newspaper."

Alice could not believe her ears. Donna had just suggested two of her best ideas, the toy project and the class newspaper. It seemed as if Donna knew what she had been going to say! Alice wished that she had asked to speak first. Now she would have to think of something else to say. But what? There wasn't much time.

Alice felt Lydia, who was at the next desk, poke her in the ribs. Lydia was grinning and trying with all her might not to laugh. She poked Alice again. Alice couldn't imagine what was so funny. And she wished Lydia would stop poking her. She gave Lydia a dirty look.

"And so, fellow classmates—" Donna came to the end of her speech. She paused and took a deep breath. All of a sudden Alice heard a popping sound. Donna gasped and looked up from her speech with an expression of surprise. She turned bright red. The girls sitting at the sides of the classroom giggled. Then Alice saw what had happened. Donna's skirt had fallen down around her ankles. The waist button had popped off. The class was in an uproar. Alice glanced at Lydia, who made a victory sign.

"What's going on, Lydia?" Alice whispered.

"You see! Pranks work!" Lydia was triumphant. "When Donna was at her locker this morning, I told her her skirt was unbuttoned and I'd button it. But what I really did was cut the threads with a pair of scissors I had in my bag. I just knew it would pop off!"

Alice smiled in spite of herself, although she did think Lydia had gone too far that time. She would speak to her later.

"Now, girls, I want quiet!" Mrs. Parker fished in the depths of her vast black handbag. She pulled out a safety pin and handed it to Donna.

"Accidents will happen," Mrs. Parker said, trying to calm down the class. "I think we should all give Donna a nice round of applause for a fine speech."

Mrs. Parker clapped. The girls joined in. Donna disappeared behind the lectern as she bent down to retrieve her skirt. She bobbed back up, fastened her skirt with the safety pin, and headed back to her desk. Her face was still red, but Alice had to admit that she walked with dignity.

"Now it's Alice's turn," said Mrs. Parker. Alice hesitated. She took a deep breath, stood up, and walked to the lectern. She pretended she had a book on her head to make her stand straight. As for the speech, she hoped that inspiration would come at the last minute.

"My speech will be short and simple," Alice began, remembering that her father always complained about long speeches at business meetings. Besides, she didn't really have much to say. Donna had already used her good ideas. "I can only say that I agree wholeheartedly with what Donna has said about the importance of school spirit and class spirit. And, like Donna, I would do everything I could to encourage both." Alice hesitated. Some of the girls were looking bored. Hilary actually yawned. Jane stared at a small cardboard box in her lap. Kathy played with a paper clip, straightening it out. Sarah and Lydia looked worried. Alice felt herself losing her audience.

"School spirit is the force that makes Miss Barton's special. But—but—" she repeated dramatically, "school spirit by itself is not enough. What we need is *inter*-school spirit." Alice noted some puzzled expressions, but she pressed on, feeling inspired at last. "Miss Barton's does not exist in a vacuum. We live in a great city, and Miss Barton's is one school among many. If I am elected president, I plan to increase our contacts with other schools, particularly with—" Alice paused and caught the eyes of her audience— "*boys*' schools." She had them now. Marina was riveted.

"Just think, my fellow classmates, of the advantages of organizing inter-school plays. Girls would no longer have to play boys' parts! Think of the advantages of inter-school cooperation. I agree with Donna that starting a class newspaper is a good idea, but why limit it to our fifth grade? We could invite students from other schools to contribute articles. We could have roving reporters, particularly in *boys*' schools.

"As for our class project, collecting toys is an excellent idea. But I suggest that we hold an *inter*-school party and have a toy as the admission fee." Alice was in her stride. She knew that she had the full attention of the class, and she was enjoying the feeling.

"So, promoting inter-school spirit would be my main goal as class president. But that is not all. I would also like to improve life at Miss Barton's as well. And I would start with school lunches." Alice knew she had picked another good subject. Everyone complained about the lunches. There had even been an occasional cockroach in the cold salads. "What we need are more choices. For example, why can't we have apple juice as well as milk?" Alice noticed that Kathy was definitely paying attention. "Why can't we—"

A chorus of screams interrupted Alice's speech. The next thing Alice knew, girls were jumping up on their desks and shrieking, pointing wildly at the floor. Mrs. Parker stood up. She rapped her ruler on the desk and demanded silence. Then she, too, leaped up onto her chair. Sometimes it was handy for a teacher to wear bright green running shoes, Alice decided. Following the pointing fingers, Alice saw several black water bugs scurrying across the floor. They seemed to be coming from under Jane's desk.

What a bunch of sissies, thought Alice. *Afraid of water bugs!* But where had they come from? Was it a plot? Only Jane sat calmly at her desk. So that was it! Alice detected a slight smile on Jane's lips. Then she remembered Jane telling everyone about her bug collection. She would go down to the laundry room in the basement of her

apartment building and collect roaches and water bugs. So that was how she had managed this,
Alice told herself angrily.

Mrs. Parker was not pleased, either. She
pulled herself together and climbed down from
her chair. With her hands on her hips, she ad-
dressed the class. "This is a disgrace!" Her face
was twisted and a sort of purplish color. "A disgrace!" she repeated. Gradually the girls quieted
down. The water bugs had disappeared behind
the radiators and bookshelves.

"First Donna's skirt, and now this! It's too
much. Too many 'accidents.' I am disappointed in
the entire fifth grade. I think that you have failed
to understand the principles of democratic elections." Mrs. Parker was back to her usual color,
but she was still angry. "Freedom of speech is
guaranteed by the first amendment of the
Constitution. Men fought and died so that we
Americans might elect, by *democratic* process,
government officials who can rule our country
without fear or coercion.

"It is obvious to me that both sides in this
election have interfered with the basic rights of a
democratic society. I hold Donna and Alice responsible. Leaders are responsible for the actions
of their followers. I am dismayed and disappointed in all of you." Her gaze rested on
Donna and then on Alice.

Alice thought Mrs. Parker really did look
disappointed. She felt ashamed and stared at her
lap.

"Unless Alice and Donna assure me that they will stop interfering with each other's campaigns, I will cancel the election on Monday. It may be that this class is too immature to appreciate the seriousness of the democratic process. This would, of course, be the first time in the whole history of Miss Barton's that a fifth grade had failed to elect class officers."

Alice felt awful. She would talk to Donna. The honor of the fifth grade was at stake. *Her* honor was at stake. She had suspected all along that pranks were a bad idea. Mrs. Parker was right. Lydia had gotten out of hand. A meeting with Donna was necessary. A summit meeting! Sarah could be her emissary.

The bell rang. It was not too soon for Alice. She had a lot to do.

CHAPTER NINE

Summit in the Third-Floor Bathroom

By lunchtime Alice had arranged the meeting. She, Sarah, and Lydia were waiting in the bathroom when Donna and Jane entered. Hilary wasn't there. She had a violin lesson right after lunch, and she needed some extra time to practice.

"I suspected all along that pranks were not the best way to win an election," Alice started. "Though it is clear to me that Donna has been involved in mischief of her own. Otherwise, how do we explain the water bugs?"

"But—but—" protested Donna and Jane in unison.

"The meeting is called to order," Lydia announced. "I think we should agree to let each candidate speak for one minute. In that time she will make suggestions. Also, we don't have much time; we still have to eat lunch. Obviously we have displeased 'the Parker.' Alice will begin."

Alice stepped forward. "As I said before, pranks don't pay."

"You started them," Donna interrupted. "Don't tell me my skirt fell off by accident. Lydia had something to do with it."

"What about the water bugs? I saw Jane with that box. And, besides, you said what I was going to say. Did you read my speech?"

"Certainly not!"

"Then someone must have *told* you what was in it."

"Aha! I knew it!" declared Lydia. "A spy! Counterespionage! Worse yet, there's a Mole in our organization!"

"A what?" Sarah asked.

"Mole. M-O-L-E. You know, the animal that bores tunnels in the ground. That's what they call spies who pretend to be on your side when they aren't. They have them in all the best spy movies."

"Oh," said Sarah. "But that's terrible! Who could it be?"

Alice and Sarah and Lydia looked from one to the other. And then from Donna to Jane.

"Don't look so smug, Donna," Alice said. "This is supposed to be a serious meeting."

"So what?" Jane interrupted. "A good leader never reveals the identity of her secret agents."

"Then you admit it."

"I admit nothing."

"But you're supposed to cooperate," Sarah

pointed out. "That's why Alice called this meeting."

"Well, Alice told Marina my brother had a rash on his neck," Donna said.

"I did *not*! I said Peter *didn't* have one."

"It's the same thing."

"No, it's not."

"Who's Peter?" Jane asked.

"We are not here to discuss boys," Alice said loftily. "We are here to discuss the election."

"Well, you certainly talked about boys in your speech."

"It seems to me," Sarah said slowly, "that we had better agree to give up pranks. If we don't, Mrs. Parker will cancel the elections. We'll lose face with the sixth grade. The whole middle school will be laughing at us."

"Okay," Donna conceded. "I promise not to play any more tricks on Alice—if Alice promises, too."

"Agreed."

"Shake on it." Donna held out her hand to Alice, who took it. Jane and Sarah shook hands, too.

Lydia was crestfallen. "How could you, Alice?" she wailed after Jane and Donna had left. "My position in the organization has been undermined! I've been squeezed out!"

"Come off it, Lydia," Alice said. "I only agreed to give up pranks. We still have a lot to do. And the first item on the agenda is to identify the spy. You, Lydia, are in charge of all espionage operations, which is a very important and very sensitive post. No one is above suspicion."

Lydia beamed.

"And," Alice concluded, looking at Sarah, "we still have to deal with the Special Interest Groups."

Marina sidled up to Alice in the hot-lunch line. "Alice," she said, "I've thought about what you said about Peach loyalty."

"Gee, Marina. That's wonderful. I think it's very important for the Peaches to stick together and to honor the Peach code."

"You *did* mention Peter. You didn't forget, did you?"

"Of course not. What about Donna's brother?"

"His class is having a ski weekend, and he's going, so he can't come to the square dance. Could I meet Peter? Before I invite him, I mean."

"Of course. Next week would be a good time. *After* the election."

"Thank you, Alice."

Sarah joined Alice as Marina moved ahead to the salad bar. "What was that all about?"

"The Defector has been taken care of. You can put her back on our side of the list."

CHAPTER TEN

The Mole

Late Friday afternoon, Alice and Sarah sat on the
floor of Alice's bedroom, poring over Sarah's lists.
Alice had called an emergency meeting of her
campaign committee to discuss the problem of
the Mole. She and Sarah were waiting for Lydia
and Hilary.

Sarah was worried. "Things are tight. So far
we have gained two Turnips, Kathy and Cynthia.
And one Undecided, Dana. We need one more Undecided. We have to be sure of Marina, and we
must ferret out the Mole in our midst and persuade it—I mean her—to vote for you, Alice. Then,
we'll win by two votes."

The election hung in the balance. Alice knew
that every vote counted and that she could win or
lose by as little as one vote.

"Alice!" called Mrs. Whipple from the living
room. "Lydia is here. I just buzzed her in. Will
you please open the door when she comes up?"

Alice opened the door and found Lydia bent
over double. She was wearing a witch's mask and

65

a black pointed hat. She had stuffed something in the back of her blazer to look like a hump. She leaned on an old broom.

"Come in, Lydia. We were just getting to the Mole. Where's Hilary? I thought she was coming with you."

"She said to tell you she had an engagement with her horse. Much more important than a mere Mole!" Lydia glanced quickly over her hump and rushed inside.

"Now that we're all here," Alice said, closing her bedroom door, "I will call the meeting to order. As you know, this is an emergency meeting to discover the identity of the Mole. Lydia, since you are APES, you may speak first."

Lydia removed her mask and stuffed it inside her pointed hat. "It's an open-and-shut case," she said confidently. "Perfectly obvious."

"What's obvious?"

"Your room is bugged. That's what's obvious."

"Don't be stupid, Lydia."

"Well, how else could anyone have known what was in your speech?"

"Maybe someone read it," said Sarah. "Did you leave your speech anywhere, Alice?"

Alice thought for a moment. "Well, yesterday I brought my notes for my speech to school. I thought I might get to work on it during lunch. The notes were in my desk all day."

"What a dumb place to leave them. How can

you expect me to run a tight security network for you, Alice, if you do things like that? You should have put them in your locker and padlocked it. I really must protest—"

A knock on the door interrupted Lydia.

"Who is it?"

"Me."

"Go away, Beatrice. We're busy." Alice was still mad about the brownies.

"Well, then it's not me. It's LSOCAP."

"*SOCAP*. The *L* is silent," Lydia reminded her.

"If you don't let me in, I won't tell you what I know."

"What do you think?" Alice consulted her aides. "Shall we?"

"It might be important," Lydia pointed out.

Alice opened the door. Beatrice walked straight over to the rocking chair. She sat down and rocked back and forth. She hummed a few bars of "Yankee Doodle."

"Well?" demanded Alice. "You *did* say you wanted to tell us something."

"What will you give me?"

"Do you want to be SOCAP or not?" Having a little sister could be a big pain. "For that matter, do you want to remain an honorary Peach?"

"You can't scare me, Alice. Anyway, it *is* important. Donna's sister's baby-sitter took me and Donna's sister to the park."

"So what?"

"We played on the swings—"

"Big deal. Look, Beatrice—" Alice was losing her patience.

"She told me something."

"What?" Lydia perked up. "I knew it! A plot!"

"It's about a *Peach*."

"Which Peach?" asked Sarah.

"An *important* Peach. A *horrible* Peach."

"Look, Beatrice. Are you or are you not going to tell us which Peach? Because if you're not, get out of my room!"

"Will you give me four lemon drops?" Beatrice knew that Alice kept a store of lemon drops in her elephant-shaped bank. She got them in by twisting off the round metal slot under the elephant.

"I'll give you two."

"Three."

"Okay. Now who is it?"

"Hilary."

"What about Hilary?" asked Lydia.

"Donna's sister says Donna promised to appoint Hilary secretary-treasurer."

"So *she's* the traitor!" declared Lydia finally. "She's the Mole! I should have guessed. And to think she used to be my best friend!"

"That's precisely why I'm appointing you Mole catcher," Alice said thoughtfully. "You must make her see the light. It's a question of Peach honor and Peach loyalty. We also need her vote." Alice paused. "You'll have to get her on Monday morning, just before homeroom. That way she won't have time to change her mind before voting. You can tell her that we *know*. Tell her that we will forgive her if—and only if—she comes back to our side. You might add that I will appoint her secretary-treasurer."

"Would you? After what she's done?"

"I don't know yet. I have to promise it to someone else, too."

After Lydia and Sarah went home, and while Beatrice was busy having a shampoo, Alice decided to approach her last Special Interest Group. She dialed Claudine's number.

"Allô?"

"Oh, hello, Madame Dubois. This is Alice Whipple. May I please speak to Claudine?"

"Yes, Aleece. I will get her."

"Allô?"

"Hi, Claudine. It's Alice. I've been wondering about something. Do you have self-government in French schools? You know, class president, elections, vice-presidents, secretaries—"

"No. Not really. We have to study all the time. The teachers tell us what to do."

"You mean you don't get to vote on things?"

"No."

"I see. Well, I thought that maybe since you're in an American school for only one year, you might like to be part of the self-government system."

"Oh?"

"Yes, I thought that it would be a nice American sort of experience for you. Of course, you could never actually *be* president because you weren't *born* in America. But you could be something else. Secretary-treasurer for example."

"What do you mean, Alice?"

"*My* secretary-treasurer. In our class, whoever is elected president gets to choose the secretary-treasurer—sort of like a cabinet post in the White House. I could choose you—*if* you wanted the experience, that is. But then you would have to vote for me. Presidents always choose from their own party when they fill an important government post."

"Oh, but, Alice. This makes me—how do you call it?—embarrassed."

"It does? Why?"

"Because Donna called me yesterday. She said *she* would make me the secretary-treasurer if I voted for her. I told her I would."

"Gosh, Claudine, that's really too bad. I'm awfully sorry to have to tell you this, but she can't make you secretary-treasurer."

"She can't? But why not?"

"Because she promised it to Hilary."

"She did?"

"Yes. And there can't be more than one secretary-treasurer in the government."

"No. I suppose not."

"Exactly. So you see, you'd be better off voting for me."

As Alice replaced the receiver, she thought it

was a good thing that her spy network was so
efficient. Now that she knew what Donna was
doing, *she* could figure out how to retaliate. And,
anyway, she wasn't absolutely sure yet who she
would choose for secretary-treasurer. And she
couldn't choose until she *was* president. And
she couldn't actually *be* president unless Claudine voted for her. Alice felt better.

CHAPTER ELEVEN

Disaster Strikes

"But, Mother," Alice protested. "I don't *want* to go to the Museum of Natural History today. I have to work on my campaign."

"Nonsense, Alice. It's Saturday, and I'm taking Beatrice and James to the show at the planetarium, and I promised Peter's mother he could come along. He wants to see the big game animals, and he would prefer it if you came, too."

"Oh, all right. but I don't want to stay long."

Alice and Peter were on their own for an hour while Mrs. Whipple took Beatrice and James to the planetarium to see a program on the Milky Way.

"Let's go look at the mineral room," Alice suggested. "They have the best stones and gems and diamonds."

"Nah. That's sissy stuff. I want to see the big game animals from Africa and Asia. Come on."

"Half an hour in the mineral room first."

"If you swear we'll see the animals after."

"I swear."

The mineral room was downstairs. As they passed through one room, Alice saw a familiar-looking figure standing with her back to them. Alice was horrified. It was Marina! Alice spun around and started back the way they had come.

"Come on, Peter," said Alice, taking him by the arm.

"What do mean 'come on'? What about the minerals?"

"Sissy stuff. I changed my mind. I want to see the animals."

"You do?"

"Yes. Now let's go."

"Girls are always changing their minds," Peter remarked as he followed Alice through a maze of darkened rooms.

"Girls are supposed to be changeable. It's part of our charm," Alice reminded him.

"Well, presidents aren't."

"Oh, yes, they are. My parents say the president is always saying one thing and doing another."

"In that case, you'll be a great president."

"Oh, shut up. Come on. The animals are over here." She blinked a few times until her eyes got used to the dark.

"Oh, boy," said Peter staring up at the display of African elephants. "Look at those tusks. I bet they could really rip you apart. When I grow up, I'm going to be a big game hunter and go on safaris. Maybe I'll let you come. You could carry my equipment."

"Presidents don't carry equipment." Alice walked over to look at the zebras in a case across from the elephants. "Uh-oh," she said. It was Marina again. She was at the other end of the hall studying the rhinos.

Alice knew she had to think fast. "Listen, Peter," she whispered quickly.

"Why are you whispering?"

"Shhhh! Don't turn around. Back there in front of the rhinos is an *awful* girl in my class. Her name is, ummm, Charlotte. Trouble is, when I was telling Marina how nice you were, you know, for the square dance, Charlotte was listening. And now *she* wants to meet you. But, Peter, you don't want to meet her. She's tall and stuck-up, and all she thinks about are boys and dances. She'd chase you all over the place and insist that you take her to the dance even though she's at least six inches taller than you."

"What should I do? What if she comes over here?"

"Tell you what. You stay here. I'll go talk to her. But if you do meet her, don't tell her your name is Peter. Say it's—it's—Algernon."

"Algernon? What kind of a name is that?"

"It's a regular name. Stay here. I'll be right back."

Alice scooted over to the rhinos. "Hi, Marina," she said softly. "What brings you here?"

"Hi, Alice. My mom dropped me off while

she ran some errands. I have to leave in a few minutes to meet her on the front steps."

"Oh. Well, I did want to tell you. You see that *short* boy over there by the elephants? The one with the dark hair and freckles? I have to spend the afternoon with him. My mother promised his mother. Actually he's a friend of Peter's younger brother. I'm telling you this so you won't want to meet him. You see, I told Peter about you and the square dance. I mentioned that you were a really good actress, too. Peter's favorite subject is drama. He had the lead in his class play last year. Anyway, this friend of his brother, his name is Algernon, was listening to my conversation with Peter, and now Algernon wants to meet you, too. But he's a pest, and he'll try to take you to *his* class dance. He's the shortest boy in the class. And he's only in the fifth grade. So *if* you do meet him, be sure you don't tell him your real name. Say you're Charlotte."

"Did you tell her?" Peter asked when Alice returned.

"Yes, don't worry. As long as she thinks you're Algernon, you're safe."

"Phew!"

As Alice and Peter were talking, Marina circled the room. She was almost up to them. Alice rushed over to her. "It's okay, he thinks you're Charlotte."

They finally met in front of the mandrill case.

"Charlotte, this is Algernon. Algernon, this is Charlotte."

Marina towered over Peter. She looked down at the top of his head. "Hello," she said curtly.

"Hi, Charlotte," Peter mumbled to her chin.

Alice studied the long blue nose of the mandrill, wishing Marina would disappear.

"Oh, yoo-hooo! Alice!"

Oh, no. It was her mother with Beatrice and James. Talk about bad timing! Alice had to get to them before they said anything. She started to run toward them.

"Hi, Peter. Hi, Marina," shouted Beatrice across the marble hall. "The Muddy Way show was great!"

Alice's heart sank. She turned around. Peter and Marina were glaring at her.

CHAPTER TWELVE

The Mole Catcher

Lydia waited for Hilary on the school steps. It was exactly fifteen minutes to eight. The vote was scheduled for eight-ten in homeroom. That gave Lydia twenty-five minutes to accomplish her mission.

The minutes ticked by slowly. At twelve minutes to eight Hilary's chauffeur-driven Mercedes pulled up in front of the school.

"Hello, Hilary," Lydia greeted her as she stepped onto the curb. "I have an important message for you. It's from Alice."

"What message?" Hilary looked nervous.

"It's about the campaign—and the election."

"What about it?"

"Well, I *had* hoped you might tell me. But since you won't, I have to tell you that your cover is blown. We're on to you. We *know*."

Hilary gulped.

Lydia decided to soften her approach. That's what they did in all the espionage movies—first threats, then promises. "Look, Hilary, we know that deep down you are a loyal and true Peach. Everyone makes mistakes. We're prepared to forgive and forget."

"You are?" Hilary's forehead wrinkled.

"Yes. But we can't discuss this here. Too public. Meet me in the fourth-floor broom closet at five minutes to eight. And don't be late. Wait," she added quickly. "Let's synchronize our watches. Time is of the essence. Don't forget the password."

Five minutes later Lydia was sitting once again on an upside-down water bucket in the dark closet. She was not the least bit nervous this time. Just a matter of practice, she thought. Jane Bond! It had a nice ring to it.

There was a knock at the door. "A for P," Hilary whispered. "A for P" was the new Peach password, short for Alice for President. Lydia opened the door, pulled Hilary in, and shut the door behind her.

"Can't we turn on the light? I can't see a thing."

"You don't have to see, Hilary. Just listen. I don't think I need to tell you how deeply disappointed, I, of all Peaches, am in you. My best friend, a traitor! I tried to defend you to the others, Hilary. I really did. It wasn't easy."

"You did, Lydia? Gosh, thanks. I didn't want to betray the Peaches. But, you see, I couldn't help it. Donna promised to make me secretary-treasurer, and Alice wouldn't. At least Donna appreciated my talent. She realized how valuable my connections could be. I wish Alice had. Then I wouldn't have had to be a spy and tell her what was in Alice's speech."

Lydia could hardly believe her ears. She did think Hilary sounded ashamed of herself, though.

"Come on, Hilary. That's the oldest trick in the book. Donna promised that post to more than one person. That's the way politics works. You should know better. Campaign promises are one thing and what happens once someone is elected is another matter."

"But Donna *could* appoint me, couldn't she? Even if she promised it to others?"

"That's no excuse, Hilary. You know that. But, as I said, we are prepared to forgive and forget. Alice knows what a hard worker you are. She is, in fact, prepared to offer you the post of secretary-treasurer *if* you give your solemn word never to defect from the ranks of Peaches again. What do you say?"

"I never wanted to defect in the first place, Lydia. And I never would have if my talents had been appreciated." Hilary was back to her old self again, thought Lydia.

"But now that Alice has finally recognized my true value, I promise to be loyal."

"Good," said Lydia. "We're late for class."

Her digital watch glowed in the dark. "We'd better get to homeroom."

Lydia groped for the doorknob. She tried to turn it. It wouldn't budge. She couldn't open the door!

CHAPTER THIRTEEN

The Election

When Alice entered the classroom, she straightened her shoulders. *Presidents have good posture,* she thought. *Except for the really tall ones like Abraham Lincoln and Andrew Jackson.* Even without Marina, Alice knew that she had one more vote than Donna. It was too bad that the election was going to be so close. When she was president, Alice decided that she would stress class unity and go out of her way to be nice to Turnips.

"Congratulations," whispered Sarah, making a quick victory sign as Alice passed. Alice smiled and sat down. She lifted her desk top and straightened out her books and pencils. Almost everyone was seated now. Mrs. Parker arrived. It was just eight. Alice lowered her desk top and looked up. Marina glared at her and then turned to smile at Donna. The bell rang.

"*Good* morning, girls," Mrs. Parker said, beaming.

But Alice was not listening. Something was

terribly wrong. The desk next to hers was empty. Lydia hadn't arrived. Where was she?

"Election day has arrived at last," continued Mrs. Parker. "And in spite of our little problems, I think you *have* come to understand the principles of a democratic government and the procedures of a democratic election. A government 'of the people, by the people, and for the people,' which is the basis of our system. And it is this system that has provided the model for our class elections at Miss Barton's. Today you are going to cast your ballots, but before you do, I want to go over the voting procedure."

Alice looked around the classroom. Another desk was empty. Hilary's! Alice felt a growing sense of panic. Lydia *and* Hilary! What could have happened to them?

Mrs. Parker stood up and began passing out ballots. "As you will see, girls, there are two slates on the ballot. The A slate is marked 'Alice for President and Sarah for Vice-President.' The B slate consists of Donna and Jane. You will each put a cross in the A or B box. I think that's clear. Are there any questions?"

No one said anything.

Mrs. Parker handed Alice a ballot. "What has happened to Lydia?" Mrs. Parker asked. "And Hilary, too? Has anyone seen them, or are they both absent today?"

"I know they're here somewhere," said Alice desperately.

Mrs. Parker distributed the ballots to the

rest of the class. "They're not usually late. It would be a shame for them to miss the election."

Not nearly so much of a shame for them as for me, thought Alice. *They must have heard the bell. But why aren't they here? I bet I know where they are.*

"After you mark your ballots, I want you to fold them and put them in these two boxes, which Toni and Elizabeth will pass around." Mrs. Parker held up two empty tissue boxes that she had covered with aluminum foil.

A fire drill! thought Alice. That would give her time. She prayed that the bell would ring. Why was it always during lunch or gym or recess and *never* when you needed it? Like during math class or tests or *now!* Maybe she should stand up and yell "Fire!" That was the way people in old movies started a panic. All she needed was a short panic. Just enough time to get to the fourth-floor broom closet and see what was going on. She needed those two votes!

Alice saw that Donna had a distinct smirk on her face. So did Marina.

Mrs. Parker returned to her desk. "Well, girls, I think we'd better start if we are going to get the vote collected and counted before the end of homeroom."

A bomb scare! That would do it, thought Alice. Last year before, when Miss Barton's had had a bomb scare, the whole school had to be evacuated into the garage across the street. Hilary had acted like such a crybaby, Alice re-

membered. The teachers had had to send her to
the nurse because she was so upset. And the
bomb squad came to search the building. It was
very exciting and time consuming. Maybe the
bomb squad would look in the fourth-floor broom
closet and find Hilary and Lydia.

"Toni and Elizabeth," Alice heard Mrs.
Parker say. "When all the ballots are in the
boxes, bring them up to my desk, please."

Alice gazed out of one of the tall classroom
windows overlooking the East River. She could
see a piece of wood swirling along in the current.
The windows were open. Alice felt a draft of air.

If only a pigeon would fly in. Or better yet,
Peter Pan. Why couldn't he fly in a classroom
window? It didn't have to be a bedroom. There
was even a Wendy in the class.

Toni held out the ballot box to Alice. Alice
looked up in surprise. She hadn't even marked
her ballot yet. She quickly put an X in the A box,
folded the paper, and stuffed it in the box. Unless
a miracle happened, and Alice didn't think it
would, she was not going to be president of the
fifth grade.

Toni and Elizabeth finished collecting the
ballots. Alice watched as Mrs. Parker took them
out of the boxes, unfolded them, and placed them
in two neat piles on her desk.

A typhoon! That would do it! A sudden blast
of air and the ballots would go flying around the
classroom like Dorothy's house in *The Wonderful*

Wizard of Oz. Mrs. Parker wouldn't even be able to get hold of the ballots, let alone count them.

"Well," said Mrs. Parker, looking up and smiling. "The vote is in. The fifth grade has a president and a vice-president."

Alice stared at the classroom door, willing it to burst open and reveal Lydia and Hilary.

"The count stands at—"

Maybe, Alice thought, if she stood up and pretended to faint . . .

"Eleven votes for Alice and Sarah and twelve votes for Donna and Jane. I hereby announce that the president of the fifth grade is Donna Ellington."

It was all over.

Alice resigned herself to her defeat. As she thought about it, she realized that she could have run a much better campaign. She certainly had messed up things with Marina and Peter. And she *had* allowed Lydia to get out of hand. *And* she hadn't managed Hilary very well, either. But then, it was important to learn from one's mistakes. Anyway, all was not lost yet.

CHAPTER FOURTEEN

Alice's Last Maneuver

At exactly 8:30 A.M. the elevator stopped at the fourth floor. The lady who ran the elevator poked her head out the door to see if anyone had rung. They hadn't. But she became aware of an unusual noise about halfway down the hall. She locked the elevator into the "hold" position and went to investigate. The noise was coming from the broom closet. The closet door was closed, but it seemed to be thumping. The elevator lady heard muffled voices inside.

"Who's there?" she called out, eyeing the door with suspicion.

"Help! Help! Let us out!"

"Hold on, I'm coming. What are you doing in there?" This time the elevator lady cupped her hands at the side of the door and spoke through them.

"It's Lydia! And Hilary! The door is stuck!"

After some tugging by the elevator lady and pushing by Lydia and Hilary, the door burst open.

86

"Gosh," Lydia gasped. "It must have jammed. We're late. Thanks so much for helping us out." Lydia took Hilary by the hand and hurried her down the stairs to homeroom.

Mrs. Parker demanded to know why Lydia and Hilary had missed the election and how they had wound up in a broom closet on the fourth floor. The teachers at Miss Barton's were very strict about being late to class. But when Lydia launched into an elaborate explanation of how she and Hilary took a wrong turn and lost track of what floor they were on and confused the doors and were so busy talking that they didn't realize they were in the broom closet until it was too late, Mrs. Parker sighed and decided to drop the subject.

Lydia did not have such an easy time with Alice.

"What on earth were you doing in there?" Alice demanded later in the day. "Do you realize that we *lost* the election? All because two of my crucial votes were absent. And where were they? Locked in the broom closet? On the fourth floor? Please explain yourself."

"It was a necessary security precaution, Alice. It really was. What if someone had overheard us?"

Alice realized that Lydia had gotten carried away, and she also knew that she herself was partly to blame. Next year, when she ran for president of the sixth grade, she would do things differently.

But for now, Alice had one more detail to take care of.

She ran into Donna on the way to French class.

"Donna," Alice said, "I haven't had a chance to congratulate you yet. I think you'll make a wonderful president, and I think Jane will be a big help as vice-president. I really agreed with what you said about class spirit. It's so important for the fifth grade to stick together, just as you said. After all, we're going to be classmates until we graduate from high school. And who knows, maybe we'll even go to the same college."

"Gee, Alice. That's awfully nice of you."

"Thank you, Donna. You know, I was just thinking—"

"Yes?"

"I *do* have a whole block of votes. Even though I *did* lose. I thought maybe since you thought class spirit was so important, you'd like my block on your side."

"What a good idea, Alice. That's very generous of you."

"Our class could be a model for the whole school. We could vote unanimously on all your good ideas, class projects, the newspaper, the toys. Your year as president would stand out as an inspiration in the long and distinguished history of Miss Barton's School."

"Gosh, Alice. Do you really think so?"

"Definitely. Of course, you *would* need help."

"What kind of help?"

"Well, *if* you appointed *me* secretary-treasurer . . ."

ABOUT THE AUTHORS

LAURIE ADAMS is the coauthor of *Alice and the Boa Constrictor*. In addition, she has written three books on art as well as articles on art history and psychology. She is a professor of art history at the City University of New York and a psychoanalyst in private practice. She lives with her husband and their two children in New York City.

ALLISON P. COUDERT is the coauthor of *Alice and the Boa Constrictor*. She is also the author of a book on the history of alchemy and early chemistry. She teaches at the State University of New York. She has one daughter and lives in New York City.